MW01103582

Ben Over Night

For Anneke, Henk and Grace, my neighbours

—*Sarah*

for Tyson and Keelan

—*Kim*

Published in Canada by Fitzhenry & Whiteside,
195 Allstate Parkway, Markham, Ontario L3R 4T8

Published in the United States by Fitzhenry & Whiteside,
121 Harvard Avenue, Suite 2, Allston, Massachusetts 02134

www.fitzhenry.ca godwit@fitzhenry.ca
10 9 8 7 6 5 4 3 2 1

Library and Archives Canada Cataloguing in Publication

Ellis, Sarah
Ben over night / Sarah Ellis; illustrations by Kim La Fave.

ISBN 1-55041-807-6

I. LaFave, Kim II. Title.

PS8559.L57B45 2005 jC813'.54 C2004-906851-2

U.S. Publisher Cataloging-in-Publication Data
(Library of Congress Standards)

Ellis, Sarah.
Ben over night / Sarah Ellis; illustrations by Kim La Fave.
[32] p. : col. ill. ; cm.
[32] p.: col. ill.; cm.
Summary: Ben loves to play at his best friend's house, but when it's time for a sleepover all Ben can think about is going home. Ben's brother and sister try some creative solutions to help their younger sibling get over his fear.

ISBN 1-55041807-6
1. Sleep – Fiction. 2. Bedtime – Fiction. I. La Fave, Kim. II. Title.
[E] 22 PZ7.E55Be 2005

Fitzhenry & Whiteside acknowledges with thanks the Canada Council for the Arts, the Government of Canada through the Book Publishing Industry Development Program (BPIDP), and the Ontario Arts Council for their support of our publishing program.

Design by Wycliffe Smith

Printed in Hong Kong

Ben Over Night

by Sarah Ellis
Illustrated by Kim LaFave

Fitzhenry & Whiteside

Ben lives kitty-corner to Peter. Ben and Peter are best friends.

Ben can be almost anything at Peter's house.

He can be a pirate.

He can be a musician.

He can be a cook.

He can be a potato.

He can be lighter than air.

He can be invisible.

The one thing that Ben can't be at Peter's house is a sleepover-nighter.

Ben would like to have a sleepover
at Peter's.

Ben's brother Joe goes
to sleepovers where he
makes his own pizza
and dyes his hair green.

Ben's sister Robin goes to camp
where she toasts marshmallows
and sleeps in a tent.

But when Ben goes to sleep over at Peter's, he wakes up in the middle of the night. He is in a funny bed. There are strange night noises. There is no cat on his stomach. The air isn't right.

He cries.

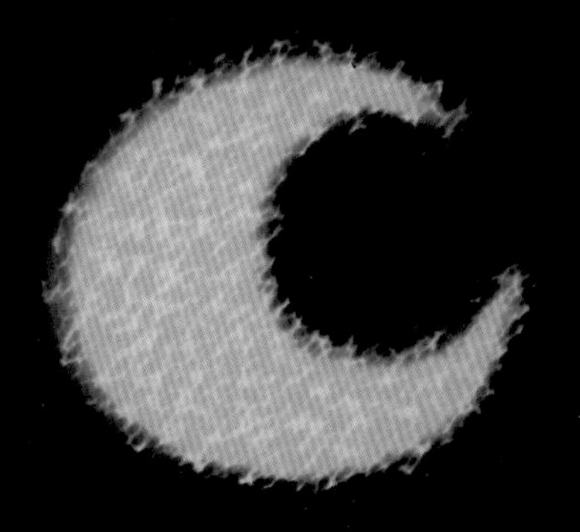

Dad comes
and takes him home.

Mum says, "Maybe you were scared
of the dark. You need a flashlight."

Dad says, "Maybe you were lonely. You
need Blankey."

Next time Ben takes a flashlight and Blankey. He cries anyway.

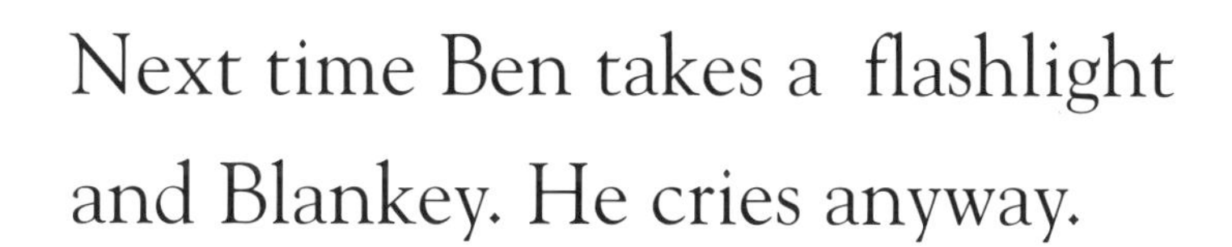

Joe says, “Maybe you’re too little. You need me!”

Ben does not want Joe to sleep over at Peter’s. Ben decides to give up on being a sleepover-nighter.

Then Robin asks Ben some questions. "What's the fastest way to get from Peter's house to our house?"

"Running?" says Ben.

"That's fast. But what's faster?"

"Driving?" says Ben.

"That's fast. But what's faster?"

"Flying?" says Ben.

"That's super- fast," says Robin. "But is it the fastest? Think about it."

Ben decides to give the sleepover one more try. He and Peter play hard hard hard.

They walk the plank.
They feed the hungry hordes.

They raise the rafters.

They tone and toughen.

They defy gravity.

They disappear.

Then they go to bed.

Ben lies in the funny bed and thinks
about all the fast Bens he could be.

Marathon Ben sprinting home.

Race car Ben driving home.

Bird Ben winging his way home.

Ben yawns.
Ben sleeps.
Snooze-Boy Ben
dreaming himself
home.

Ben wakes up
when Peter tickles
his foot. It is morning.
Night is over. Sleep is over.
The sleepover is over.

Ben bounces out of bed. He chases Peter around the room. He roars like a fast, fierce, over-nighter jungle beast.

Ben can be anything at Peter's house.